This book belongs to

_____

_____

_____

Age_____

©1992 Grandreams Books Limited.
This edition published in 2001

Adaptations from the original stories by Anne Mckie
Illustrated by Ken Mckie

Published by Grandreams Books Limited,
4 North Parade, Bath
BA1 1LF, England.

Printed in China

Favourite Tales in this book

GULLIVER'S TRAVELS

This is the story of Lemuel Gulliver, a man who lived about two hundred and fifty years ago. He studied very hard and after many years, he became a doctor. He longed to travel and loved the sea, so he became a doctor on board a sailing ship.

One day he set off on a long voyage to the South Seas on a ship called the Antelope – and here begins one of the strangest adventure stories ever told.

All went well on the Antelope for the first few weeks. Then suddenly one night, a great storm sprang up, the ship hit a rock and was wrecked.

Although the sea was rough and the waves high, Gulliver was such a strong swimmer that he managed to reach the shore. Completely exhausted, he dragged himself up the beach as far away from the sea as possible. He lay down on the first grassy bank he found and fell into a deep sleep.

At daybreak, when he opened his eyes, he tried to sit up and look around - but he was tied to the ground! He couldn't move his arms or legs or even lift his head.

Then Gulliver felt something alive running up his legs and across his chest – like a crowd of mice or several beetles perhaps!

All at once, Gulliver let out a great roar of surprise. For standing on his chest were at least forty men, each about six inches high. Gulliver's great roar startled the little men. Quickly they slid down to the floor below, where great crowds of tiny people were assembled.

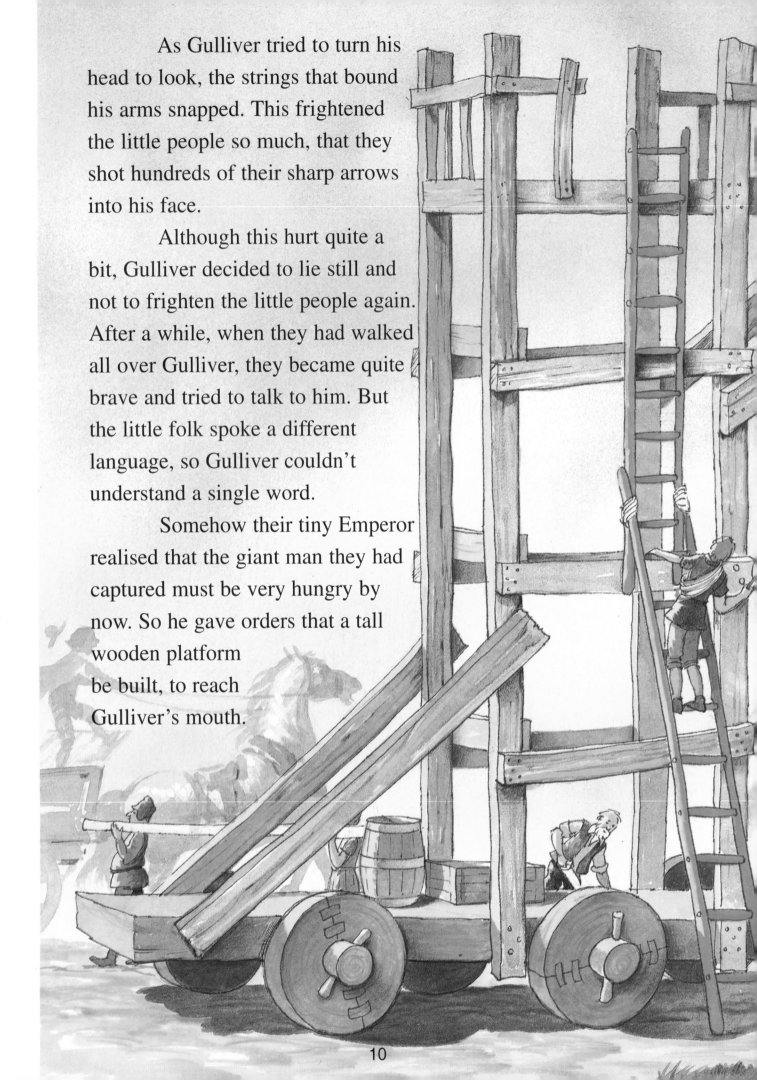

As Gulliver tried to turn his head to look, the strings that bound his arms snapped. This frightened the little people so much, that they shot hundreds of their sharp arrows into his face.

Although this hurt quite a bit, Gulliver decided to lie still and not to frighten the little people again. After a while, when they had walked all over Gulliver, they became quite brave and tried to talk to him. But the little folk spoke a different language, so Gulliver couldn't understand a single word.

Somehow their tiny Emperor realised that the giant man they had captured must be very hungry by now. So he gave orders that a tall wooden platform be built, to reach Gulliver's mouth.

After a while several cartloads of food and wine arrived. And hundreds of the tiny men climbed up the platform with baskets of bread and meat. The hungry Gulliver drank a whole barrel of their wine in one gulp, and ate a basket full of loaves in one bite.

The Lilliputians (for that is what the little people were called) kept bringing more and more until Gulliver was so full up he fell fast asleep.

The little people seemed to have lost all fear of
the gigantic Gulliver, so while he slept, thousands of
them set to work. Five hundred carpenters made a
platform on wheels, and nine hundred men hoisted the
sleeping Gulliver onto it. Then with five hundred
guards either side and one thousand five hundred
horses pulling hard, they began to move him towards
their capital city.

It took a whole day and night to reach their
destination. At last the procession came to a halt
outside a large church, which was to be Gulliver's
house – although it seemed as small as a dog kennel
to him.

The tiny Emperor of Lilliput did not intend to
set Gulliver free altogether. He ordered all his
blacksmiths to make a thick chain and padlock it onto
Gulliver's leg, so he could move around – but not very far.

News soon spread of the giant the Emperor had captured. People flocked in from all over the land of Lilliput, until the city was jammed with the little folk.

Six hundred of them were chosen to look after Gulliver, and four hundred tailors were kept busy making him new clothes. Six of Lilliput's finest scholars were sent to teach him their language.

13

At last the Emperor could understand Gulliver when he asked to be set free. He finally agreed, on one condition. Gulliver must empty his pockets of anything that could be dangerous to Lilliput.

Out came a knife, a comb and a razor. The little people were fascinated. Then came his handkerchief – which to them looked like a carpet. His snuffbox seemed like a huge chest of gunpowder; his watch made more noise than a watermill, and they thought that his purse was a fishing net.

Finally Gulliver took out his pistol and fired it into the air. So great was the noise, thousands of the little people fell flat on their backs with shock. Only the Emperor stood his ground. For a man only six inches high, he was very brave.

But even the brave Emperor feared something. And one day he came to ask Gulliver's help.

On the nearby island of Blefuscu lived people called the Big-Endians. Their fleet of fifty ships had just set sail to invade Lilliput.

What a shock the poor Big-Endian sailors got when Gulliver waded out to sea, roped all their ships together, and dragged them back to Lilliput.

It didn't take Gulliver very long to realise that the Emperor of Lilliput was only using him to fight his battle for him, and that the Big-Endians were not a wicked people at all. So Gulliver made up his mind to go over to their island and live with them.

He took a large warship from Lilliput, loaded it up with his clothes (so they wouldn't get wet), then towed it behind him to their island of Blefuscu.

He was most kindly received by the little folk, but all Gulliver really wanted was to get back to England.

Quite by chance as Gulliver was walking on the top of the cliff, he saw something floating in the sea. He could hardly believe his eyes – it was a full size rowing boat floating upside down.

Straight away the Emperor of the Big-Endians sent every ship in his fleet out to sea to tow it back to shore.

It took two thousand men to turn the boat right side up and then begin to repair it. Five hundred people stitched day and night to make the sails. Everyone on the island worked hard until the boat was ready.

Gulliver took on board several tiny live sheep and cows to take back home. Then sadly came the time to say farewell.

After only two days at sea, Gulliver was picked up by a sailing ship heading for England. When he told his strange story, the captain could hardly believe it – until he saw the tiny cows and sheep which Gulliver placed on the table in front of him.

At last Gulliver returned home. People were delighted to welcome him back, and never tired of hearing his strange story.

THE FROG PRINCE

Once upon a time there lived a King who had several beautiful daughters, but the youngest was even more beautiful than the rest.

Near the castle of the King was a large and gloomy forest. Just a short walk into the trees was a small clearing. At the far side stood an old lime tree, and beneath its branches splashed a fountain in the middle of a dark deep pool.

Whenever it was very hot, the King's youngest daughter would run off into this wood and sit by the pool, throwing her golden ball into the air. This was her favourite pastime.

One afternoon when the Princess threw the ball high up in the air – she didn't catch it! It slipped through her fingers onto the grass. Then it rolled past her into the fountain, and disappeared beneath the water.

The princess peered into the pool, but her precious golden ball was gone. Quickly, she plunged her arms into the pool as far as she could reach, but she could feel nothing except weeds and water lilies. Some people said the pool was so deep it had no bottom. So when the Princess realised her golden ball was gone forever, she began to cry. "Come back to me this minute, golden ball," sobbed the Princess, staring hard into the water.

Now as a rule, Princesses are used to getting their own way. So after her golden ball didn't magically pop up out of the water, she started to howl even louder. Dear, oh dear! First she stamped her feet and then she threw herself down on the grass in temper.

The Princess was making so much noise, that she didn't notice a big green frog stick his head out of the water and jump onto the grass beside her. "Don't cry beautiful Princess," the frog croaked. "I saw your golden ball fall into the water, and it will be my pleasure to dive down and get it for you – if you will give me something in return."

At this the Princess cheered up. "I will gladly give you my jewels and pearls, even my golden crown, if you will bring back my golden ball." It's true to say that promises should never be made in a hurry, even by Princesses, because a promise is a thing that must be kept – especially to frogs!

The frog hopped nearer to the Princess. "Pearls and jewels and golden crowns are no use to me," he went on, "but if you'll love me and be my friend, if you'll let me eat from your golden plate, drink from your golden cup, and sleep on your golden bed, I will dive down and fetch your ball."

So eager was the Princess to see her golden ball once more, that she didn't listen too carefully to what the frog had to say. "I promise you all you ask, if only you will bring back my ball."

Quick as a flash, the frog jumped into the pool then bobbed up again with the ball in his mouth. Straight away the King's daughter snatched her ball and ran back to the castle.

"Take me with you," cried the frog. "I cannot run as fast as you and shall be left behind."

But the Princess didn't care about her promise and soon forgot all about the frog. Later that day, when the Princess was sitting at the table, something was heard coming up the marble stairs, "Splish, splosh." The sound came nearer and nearer and a voice cried, "Let me in, youngest daughter of the King."

The Princess jumped up to see who had called her. Now when she caught sight of the frog, she turned very pale.

"What does a frog want with you?" demanded the King, looking rather surprised.

The Princess hung her head. "When I was sitting playing by the fountain my golden ball fell into the water. This frog fetched it back for me – because I cried so much." The Princess started to cry again. "I promised to love him and let him eat from my golden plate, drink from my golden cup and sleep on my golden bed."

The King looked at the frog and thought for a while before he spoke. "Then you must keep your promise, my daughter."

The Princess knew she must obey, so she beckoned the frog to come inside. The frog hopped in after her and jumped into her chair and straight onto the table. "Now push your golden plate near me," said the frog, "so that we may eat together." As she did so, the frog leapt onto her plate and gobbled up all her dinner, which was just as well, because the Princess didn't feel much like eating.

Next, the frog drank from her little golden cup until it was quite empty. Somehow the Princess didn't feel thirsty either! After the frog had finished, he took one great leap and landed on the Princess's knee. "Go away you ugly cold frog!" she screamed. "I will never let you sleep on my lovely clean bed!"

This made the King very angry. "This frog helped you when you needed it. Now you must keep your promise to him."

"I am very tired after that wonderful meal," the frog said, "and you did promise that I could go to sleep on your golden bed."

Very unwillingly the Princess picked up the frog and carried him upstairs to her room.

When the frog hopped into the middle of her golden bed, it was just too much for the Princess. She tugged hard at the coverlet and tipped the poor frog onto the floor.

As he fell he was changed into a handsome Prince. A spell had been cast on him by an evil witch and only the Princess had the power to break it.

The Princess was speechless. She felt very sorry indeed that she had been so unkind to the frog.

After a while, the handsome Prince and the Princess got married, and I'm sure lived happily ever after.

CINDERELLA

Once upon a time, there lived a Baron whose wife died, leaving him to bring up their little girl.

A few years later, when his daughter had grown into a beautiful young lady, the Baron married again. But sadly, soon after, he became ill and died.

His second wife was mean and cruel with a very nasty temper. And to make matters worse, she had two daughters of her own who were even worse than she was. One was very fat, one was very thin and both of them were extremely ugly. In fact, people called them the Ugly Sisters – behind their backs of course!

After the Baron's death, his daughter was treated like a servant by the stepmother and her two ugly girls. They forced her to do all the rough work in the house. The poor girl toiled from dawn to dusk, scrubbing floors and washing greasy pots and pans.

The hardest job of all was cleaning out the many fire-grates in the castle. The cinders and soot marked the girl's dress, her hands got grubby and there were black smudges on her nose. That is why the Ugly Sisters unkindly nicknamed her Cinderella.

At night, when all her work was done, Cinderella would sit by the kitchen fire warming her toes near the cinders before she went upstairs to her cold attic room.

One day at the Royal Palace the King's son announced that he was to give a splendid ball. To their great joy Cinderella's two stepsisters received an invitation. "You must make us both new ball gowns at once!" one sister yelled at Cinderella. "And do our hair to make us look more beautiful," screeched the other.

This meant that Cinderella had even more work to do. All day long she stitched and sewed. Every pleat, every frill and every bit of lace had to be just right. Not to mention the extra washing, starching and ironing of all their frilly petticoats.

In spite of all the lovely clothes Cinderella had made them, the two sisters still looked dreadfully ugly.

At last the coach arrived to take the Ugly Sisters to the ball. Not one word of thanks did Cinderella get! The nasty pair pushed and shoved their way into their seats, and drove off with their noses in the air.

Sadly, Cinderella went back into the kitchen to sit by the fire. All of a sudden, a log on the fire burst into flames filling the kitchen with light. In the brightness Cinderella noticed, for the first time, a little old lady in a cloak and pointed hat – standing right next to her.

"I am your Fairy Godmother," she said kindly, "and you are going to the ball!"

Cinderella was too surprised to speak. She had no idea she had a Fairy Godmother.

"Now quickly," the fairy said, "go into the garden and fetch me a pumpkin." Next, she told Cinderella to bring her the six mice and three rats that were caught in the trap near the kitchen cupboard. And last of all, she asked for six lizards from behind the garden shed.

With one wave of her wand the pumpkin was transformed into a glittering golden coach. The six mice turned into fine grey horses. The three rats became handsome coachmen, and lo and behold, the six lizards were smart footmen.

"Well, Cinderella, now you are ready to go to the ball," said her Godmother. "Oh dear, I almost forgot your dress!"

Once more she waved her wand and
Cinderella's ragged clothes were changed into a
magnificent silver dress which sparkled with precious
stones, and there on Cinderella's feet were a pair of
glistening glass slippers, which fitted perfectly.

As she was about to drive off in her
golden coach, her Godmother called
after her, "You must leave the ball
before the clock strikes midnight –
for my magic only lasts until then."
And with a last wave of her wand
she vanished.

Cinderella's coach was the last to arrive at the Palace. All the guests in the ballroom turned to look at Cinderella as the Prince stepped forward to greet her.

She danced so well and looked so beautiful that the Prince fell in love with her straight away.

Everyone that night was whispering about the lovely stranger who had captured the heart of the Prince. And Cinderella was so happy she lost all count of time.

All of a sudden the Palace clock struck midnight. Cinderella dashed from the ballroom as fast as she could. Halfway down the grand staircase she lost one of her glass slippers.

As she ran through the Palace gardens her wonderful ballgown turned back into rags.

No golden coach was waiting outside to take her home, instead, lying there on the ground was a pumpkin, and running away were all the mice, the rats and the six lizards.

Cinderella ran back home through the night, and hid in the dark corner of the kitchen. But when she felt in her apron pocket – she found one sparkling glass slipper.

Meanwhile, as the Prince rushed through his Palace searching for her, he found the other slipper on the stairs and picked it up. Desperately the Prince asked every guest at the ball, and all his servants, but no-one knew the name of the lovely girl.

The very next morning the glass slipper was placed on a velvet cushion and taken to the city square. "I shall marry the girl whose foot fits this glass slipper," announced the Prince.

What excitement this caused! Every girl in the kingdom wanted to try on the slipper. Princesses, serving maids, rich girls, poor girls, all tried – but it was far too small for any of them.

When it came to the Ugly Sisters' turns, they fought and squabbled about who should try it on first. They tried their hardest to squeeze their great clumsy feet into the dainty slipper – but it was no use.

All this time Cinderella had been sitting very quietly in the corner. Luckily, the Prince's servant noticed her. He placed the glass slipper on the velvet cushion in front of her. Gently she slipped it on her tiny foot – and it fitted perfectly. Then she took the other slipper from her apron pocket and, of course, they matched.

The Prince was overjoyed to find his lost love and begged Cinderella to be his bride.

The wedding was a splendid affair, with the Fairy Godmother as chief guest. The Ugly Sisters promised to mend their ways – and everyone lived happily ever after.

ALI 'BABA

Long ago in an eastern land, there lived two brothers, Cassim and Ali Baba. The elder brother Cassim married a very rich wife and didn't have to work at all.

Ali Baba, on the other hand, married a girl as poor as himself, and he had to work very hard for a living. Every day he went to the forest to look for firewood. Then he would load up his donkeys and try to sell his wood in the market place.

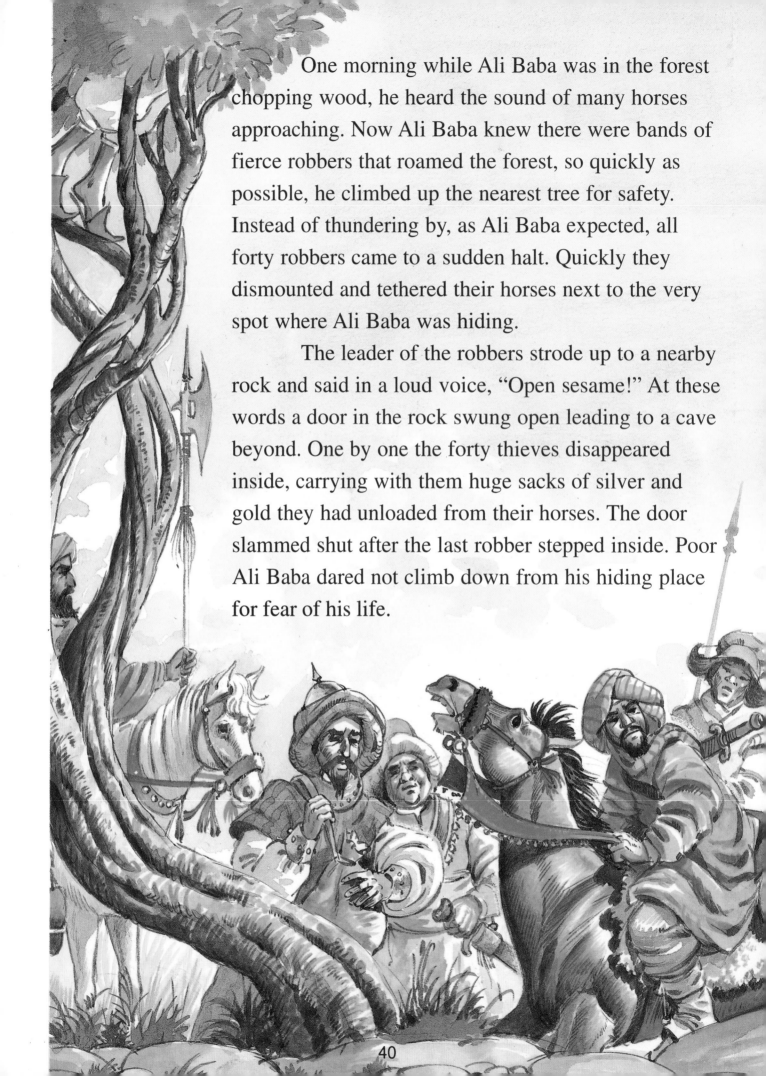

One morning while Ali Baba was in the forest chopping wood, he heard the sound of many horses approaching. Now Ali Baba knew there were bands of fierce robbers that roamed the forest, so quickly as possible, he climbed up the nearest tree for safety. Instead of thundering by, as Ali Baba expected, all forty robbers came to a sudden halt. Quickly they dismounted and tethered their horses next to the very spot where Ali Baba was hiding.

The leader of the robbers strode up to a nearby rock and said in a loud voice, "Open sesame!" At these words a door in the rock swung open leading to a cave beyond. One by one the forty thieves disappeared inside, carrying with them huge sacks of silver and gold they had unloaded from their horses. The door slammed shut after the last robber stepped inside. Poor Ali Baba dared not climb down from his hiding place for fear of his life.

After what seemed a very long uncomfortable wait, the forty thieves came out of the cave empty-handed. The robber chief raised his arms and cried, "Close sesame!" and the door in the rock shut tight. The robbers jumped back on their horses and rode away.

Plucking up all his courage, Ali Baba jumped down from the tree and ran over to the rock. "Open sesame!" he cried in a trembling voice. Straight away, the door swung open and Ali Baba found himself in a gigantic cave.

What wonders met his eyes! Sacks full of silver and gold, priceless carpets, ornaments of ivory and jade and endless chests of precious jewels. Hurriedly, Ali Baba grabbed a couple of the bags of gold, ran out of the cave, and loaded up his donkeys.

When Ali Baba's wife saw all that gold, she was overjoyed. "It is far too much to count," she whispered, quite breathless. "We must measure it into small sacks and hide it, for if we spend it a little at a time, no-one will suspect we have the robber's gold."

So off she ran to the elder brother, Cassim, to borrow a measure. This made Cassim's wife very suspicious.

"Ali Baba's wife is far too poor to need a measure," she thought to herself. So secretly she stuck a small piece of wax to the bottom, so that whatever was put in the measure would stick.

Sure enough when the measure was returned next day, one shiny gold coin was stuck to the wax. It really puzzled Cassim and his wife.

The following morning, Ali Baba set out as usual for the forest. But this time his brother Cassim was following him secretly. As soon as Ali Baba reached the rock, he uttered the magic words, "Open sesame!" The door opened and he stepped inside. Very soon he reappeared loaded down with gold and jewels.

The greedy Cassim couldn't wait to try. As soon as Ali Baba was out of sight, Cassim stood in front of the rock, "Open sesame!" he shouted, and the door opened at once. Cassim wasted no time, he rushed into the cave and began filling sacks of gold himself. But alas, when the time came for him to open the door, he'd forgotten the magic words. He tried everything but the door remained shut tight!

Later that day the robbers returned. They were such evil and cruel men that in their anger they killed Cassim and cut him up into four pieces!

Late that night when Cassim didn't return, his wife told Ali Baba how Cassim had followed him into the forest to spy on him. Ali Baba guessed what had happened. In the middle of the night he returned to the robbers' cave and found his poor dead brother just inside the entrance.

He loaded the four pieces of the body onto his donkey and returned home to break the terrible news to Cassim's wife. After much weeping, the family decided that Cassim's body must be sewn together before he could be buried (that way no-one would know he had been cut into pieces by the thieves).

A faithful family slave called Morgiana knew of an old blind cobbler who could do the task. In the dead of night she led the old man to Cassim's house. Skilfully he stitched the four pieces together, so no-one would know that Cassim had not died in his sleep. As soon as he had finished, Morgiana led the cobbler back home through the dark city streets.

Meanwhile, the forty thieves returned to their cave. When they found that Cassim's body had vanished they realised someone else knew of their hiding place. They rode into the city and began to question everyone. It wasn't long before the blind cobbler told them of his unusual task the night before.

Although he was blind, he could easily
remember the path that led to Cassim's house. The
leader of the thieves marked the door with a large
cross, so his men could return later and kill everyone
inside. But clever Morgiana came along and marked
every door in the street with a cross to confuse the
thieves, and their evil plan was foiled.

All too soon, the robber chief heard about Ali
Baba, who had once been a poor woodcutter, and was
now the richest man in the city. It didn't take him
long to guess it was Ali Baba who knew the secret of
their cave.

So the leader of the robbers disguised himself as a merchant selling oil. He called at Ali Baba's house asking for a night's lodging. With him he had a team of donkeys, each one loaded with a great jar. In every jar hid one of his evil band. Only one of the jars contained oil. That night when the household was fast asleep, the thieves planned to jump out and kill everyone.

Quite by chance, Morgiana ran out of oil for cooking. "I will borrow a little from the merchant's jar," she thought to herself.

It was then she discovered the thieves' trick. The cunning girl filled a hug pan full of oil from the jar and heated it up on the stove. When it was boiling hot she tipped some into every jar – and the forty thieves were scalded to death.

While all this was going on, Ali Baba was entertaining the robber chief, whom he had not recognised. When Ali Baba asked Morgiana to dance for his guest, she gladly agreed. As she danced she leapt forward and plunged a dagger into the robber chief's heart. It was only then that Ali Baba realised how he had been tricked, and how brave Morgiana was.

This story has a happy ending, for Morgiana was given her freedom and married Ali Baba's son. And everyone lived happily to the end of their days.

THE EMPEROR'S NEW CLOTHES

A very long time ago, there lived an Emperor who loved new clothes. He wasn't a bit like other Emperors, who spent their days ruling their people or inspecting their soldiers. This Emperor was different! His days were spent trying fancy new clothes, and admiring himself in one hundred full-length mirrors!

Every bedroom in his enormous palace was was filled from floor to ceiling with wardrobes. Every wardrobe was so packed with clothes not even the tiniest silk handkerchief would fit inside. Upstairs in the palace was bad enough, but downstairs was even worse.

All the rooms and even the corridors were full of people waiting to see the Emperor. There were tailors, weavers, shoemakers, dressmakers. Merchants with rolls of velvet and satin. Shopkeepers selling fancy shirts and frilly collars. Not to mention the jewellers! Out of their cases tumbled silver buckles, jewelled belts, sparkling rings and golden chains, each one costing a fortune.

The Emperor couldn't resist anything. He bought the lot. And to make matters worse, he told them all to come back the next day and show him more.

One day, two strangers arrived at the Emperor's palace, pretending to be weavers, "We must see the Emperor at once," shouted the two rogues, all the time trying not to laugh. For they had though of a very clever plan which could make them very rich indeed. "We must see the Emperor in secret," cried the two rogues, as they strode through the palace together.

"Clear the room and lock all the doors," the Emperor commanded as the two weavers bowed low in front of him. Excitedly they told the Emperor that they had discovered the secret of weaving magic cloth.

The Emperor looked spellbound. Then the weavers went on to explain, "To a wise and clever man like Your Majesty, the cloth is the finest ever seen – but to a fool it is completely invisible."

The Emperor could hardly believe his ears. He begged the weavers to start straight away. "Bring your loom to the palace this very day, and I will give you a bag of gold," the Emperor cried. "I must have a suit made from this magic cloth, then at last I shall be able to find out those around me who are fools."

Later that day the two weavers set up their loom in a room at the palace. They pretended to work very hard, but of course, the loom was empty. Day after day the rogues spent long hours in front of their loom – doing nothing at all! And every day they asked the Emperor for another bag of gold for payment.

Weeks passed, until the Emperor could wait no longer. "If I go myself, and I cannot see the cloth, the weavers will know I am a fool," thought the Emperor. "But if I send my Prime Minister, then I shall find out for sure if he is a fool."

Now, the Prime Minister was rather old and short-sighted. Try as he may, he could not even see one piece of thread on the loom. "I must be a complete fool," he muttered to himself. However, not wishing to lose his job he scurried off to tell the Emperor what he had found. "Magnificent, exquisite, the finest piece of cloth ever woven," he puffed, quite out of breath.

The Emperor pushed him aside. "I simply must see for myself." He ran through the palace and burst into the weavers' workroom, and all the people in his court followed him.

When the Emperor saw the empty loom he gasped, and so did everybody else. Not one of them could see a thing! As no-one wished to look a fool, they all waited for the Emperor to speak first.

He walked slowly round and round the loom thinking to himself, "I can't see a thing. I must be a fool and not fit to be Emperor."

So, he took a deep breath and faced his whole court. "It's exquisite, magnificent, quite wonderful!" he exclaimed. And everyone present, not wishing to appear foolish, congratulated the clever weavers.

"I must have the finest suit made to wear at tomorrow's parade," announced the Emperor. Then he gave the two weavers several more bags of gold, to work all night to finish the invisible suit.

The weavers could hardly believe their good fortune that the Emperor could be such a fool! The clever rogues measured the Emperor and then pretended to cut and sew the invisible cloth. At first light next morning they rushed into the Emperor's bedroom crying, "The wonderful magic suit is finished!"

The Emperor leapt out of bed, and the crafty pair pretended to help him dress in the invisible coat and breeches.

"Splendid! Absolute perfection!" the weavers exclaimed, as they stepped back to admire the Emperor.

Soon the whole court crowded round to see. But as none of them wished to appear fools, they all agreed the suit was truly magnificent. Since early morning, people had been gathering to see the Emperor's new clothes in the parade.

The word had spread quickly that only the wisest among them would see the suit. So when the Emperor paraded past wearing no clothes at all – not one of them seemed to notice. And as not one of them wished to look a fool they clapped and cheered the Emperor all through the town.

All at once a little boy in the front of the crowd pointed his finger at the Emperor and yelled, "He's got no clothes on!"

A giggle went round the crowd when they realised how stupid they had been. Poor Emperor! His face turned very red, but he held his head up high and paraded slowly back to his palace. He felt such a fool.

As for the two weavers – they left the palace rather quickly, just before the parade started – perhaps they couldn't wait to spend all that gold!

RUMPELSTILTSKIN

There was once a poor miller who had a beautiful daughter. He was so proud of her that he talked about her all day long, to anyone who would listen. "She is a bride fit for the King himself," boasted the miller to his neighbours.

How they all laughed, which made the miller brag even more. "She can even spin straw into gold!" the miller shouted at the top of his voice.

Nobody believed him, of course, except one man. He was the King's huntsman, who often rode past the mill.

On his return to the palace, the huntsman told the King about the girl who could spin straw into gold. Now the King loved gold, and when he heard the huntsman's story, he ordered the miller's daughter to be brought before him at once.

The poor girl was horrified when she knew what her father had said. But she was too afraid to tell the King her father had lied.

The King led the trembling girl into a room filled with straw. "Spin this into gold before sunrise, or you will die," ordered the King. And he locked the door behind him.

In the corner of the room was a spinning wheel. The miller's daughter took one look at it and began to weep.

All of a sudden a strange little man jumped down from a tiny window high up in the wall. He took off his cap and bowed very low. "I won't tell you my name," he grinned. "Give me your necklace and I will gladly spin all this straw into gold for you." Straight away he sat down at the spinning wheel and never stopped until every last piece of straw was turned into gold.

In the morning when the King unlocked the door, the whole room was full of gold. The dwarf, of course, was nowhere to be seen.

The King was amazed and delighted with the miller's daughter.

"May I go back home to my father now?" the poor girl begged.

The King shook his head saying, "Rest here and have some food. You have worked all night and must be tired." The miller's daughter dare not disobey the King, so she had to stay.

Now this King was very greedy, and when he saw the pile of gold, he wanted more. So that night, when the miller's daughter woke up, he led her to an even bigger room piled high with straw, and locked her inside.

Once more the girl began to weep, and once more the little man appeared, eager to begin his spinning. This time he asked for her scarf in return for his work. And the girl gladly gave it to him.

In the morning when the King unlocked the door, the room was full of gold yet again. "Spin one more room full of gold tonight," smiled the King, "and I will make you my Queen."

So that night the girl was locked in the biggest room in the palace. It was full from floor to ceiling with straw.

Yet again the dwarf appeared. "I have nothing left to give in return for your work," sobbed the miller's daughter. Then the dwarf smiled a wicked smile. "Give me your first child when you are Queen," he laughed. What could the poor girl do but agree?

The dwarf worked hard all night. In the morning his task was done, and the room was packed with gold.

The King kept his promise and married the miller's daughter, and she became his Queen. They were very happy together, especially when a little daughter was born to them.

One day the Queen sat nursing her baby, when the dwarf suddenly appeared before her. "I've come for your first born child," the dwarf cackled, jumping up and down.

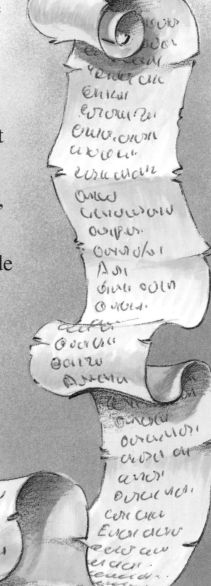

The Queen turned pale as she clutched the baby tightly in her arms. She had forgotten all about her promise to the crafty dwarf.

The Queen offered the dwarf jewels, money, anything in the whole kingdom, but he refused.

However, when she cried so bitterly, he made a bargain with her. "If you can guess my name in three days – you may keep your child."

The Queen stayed awake all night, trying to remember all the names she had ever heard. Everybody in the palace made long lists of every name they could think of.

On the first day, the dwarf came back. The Queen told him every name she knew, but after each one the dwarf shouted, "That is not my name!"

That night, the Queen secretly sent her messengers all over the land, to collect new names. When they returned to the palace at first light next day, they had brought back hundreds.

When the dwarf returned for the second time, the Queen read every name her messengers had collected. After every one, the dwarf just laughed and shook his head. Not one of them was right.

By now the Queen was distraught. Only one more day left and everyone had run out of names. Soon the dwarf would take her precious little daughter.

Long before it was light on the third day, a messenger rode into the palace courtyard demanding to see the Queen.

"I have not been able to find any new names, but I have a very strange tale to tell." He told the Queen how he had passed by a hut hidden deep in the woods. Outside the hut was a fire, round which a strange little man was singing:

"Flames dance, fire shine! Tomorrow, the Queen's child is mine. No more straw to gold I'll spin! For my name is Rumpelstiltskin!"

Can you imagine how happy the Queen was when she heard that name?

70

When the dwarf came back on the third day, the Queen pretended not to know, and guessed many names. The she said with a smile, "Could it be Rumpelstiltskin?"

The dwarf was furious, he screamed and stamped with rage. Such was his fury, that he split right in two and vanished without a trace.

The King and the miller's daughter were happy for many years. Perhaps, when the baby Princess is older, she will be told the story of the dwarf who could turn straw into gold.

THE LITTLE TIN SOLDIER

Once upon a time, there lived an old toymaker. Folk came from miles around to gaze in his shop window full of toys, and sometimes they would call in and buy presents for their children.

One day, the old toymaker melted down a very large tin spoon. Carefully he poured the hot metal into some special moulds to make a set of tin soldiers. He filled up twenty of the moulds, but on the twenty-first he ran out of tin.

So when the soldiers were turned out, twenty were exactly alike – but the very last soldier had one leg missing.

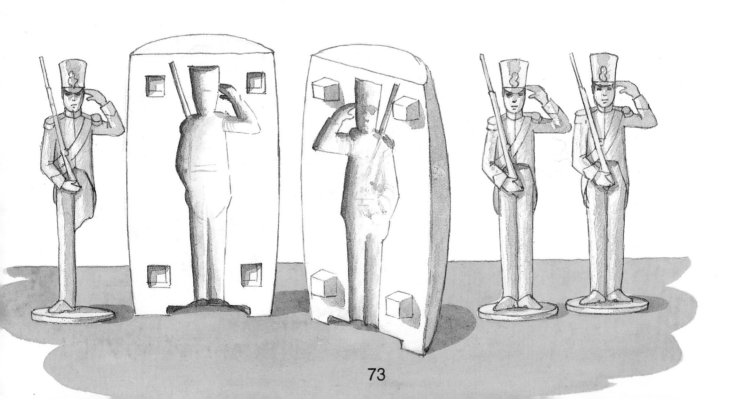

With great skill, the old toymaker painted the soldiers. He gave them red tunics and blue trousers and finished off their hats with gold braid. They looked splendid standing stiffly to attention and saluting. Even the tin soldier with one leg stood up just as straight as the others, looking every bit as brave and dashing. The old man was pleased with his work. And it wasn't too long before someone saw the twenty-one tin soldiers in his window, and bought them.

The box full of soldiers were given to a small boy for his birthday, and when he lifted the lid, he was thrilled to bits. "Tin soldiers," he gasped. "Just what I've always wanted."

The boy stood all his soldiers in a row in his nursery without even noticing that one of them had only one leg.

The little tin soldier gazed around him at the other toys. The floor below was littered with teddy bears, clockwork toys, bricks and dolls and a toy fort for the tin soldiers.

But the best toy was a splendid cardboard castle. It had tall pillars either side of the door, and more windows than the tin soldier could count. On the steps of the cardboard castle stood a graceful ballerina doll. She was balanced perfectly on one leg with the other stretched behind her – it looked as if she had only one leg.

"What a perfect wife she would make for me," sighed the little tin soldier as he gazed into her eyes. But the ballerina doll didn't even blink – she just stood there on one leg, staring back at the tin soldier. "I know that she is far too good for me," the tin soldier thought to himself. "But I must be very brave and look into her eyes until she speaks to me."

At night, when all the people in the house were asleep, the toys came out to play. The dolls and teddies danced and played games. The clockwork mice held races against the cars. Even the tin soldiers (who were supposed to be on guard) joined in the fun. But the little tin soldier and the ballerina doll just remained perfectly still and stared at each other.

Suddenly one night, the clock in the nursery struck midnight. The jack-in-the-box flew open and a bad-tempered goblin flew out. He pointed a boney finger at the tin soldier. "Stop staring at the ballerina or it will be the worse for you," he snarled.

Although the goblin gave the tin soldier a terrible fright, he bravely stood to attention and continued to gaze at the ballerina doll.

Very early next morning the little boy came into his nursery to play with his soldiers. He lined them up in a row on the window ledge, then ran off to have his breakfast.

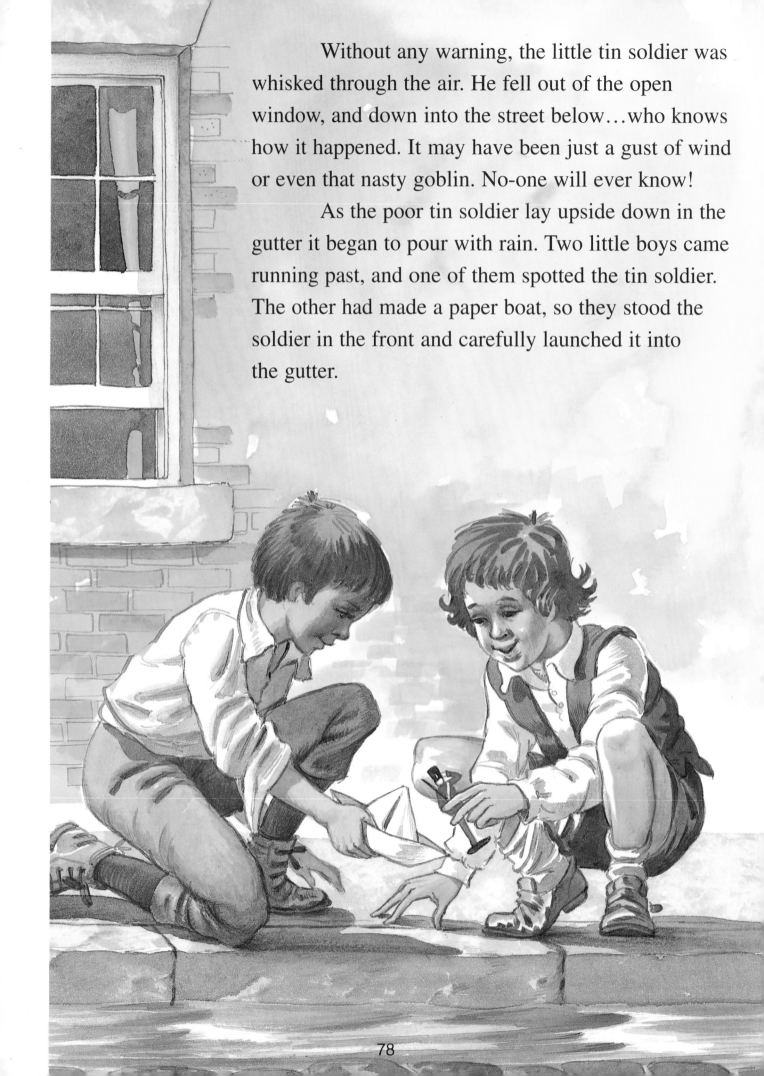

Without any warning, the little tin soldier was whisked through the air. He fell out of the open window, and down into the street below…who knows how it happened. It may have been just a gust of wind or even that nasty goblin. No-one will ever know!

As the poor tin soldier lay upside down in the gutter it began to pour with rain. Two little boys came running past, and one of them spotted the tin soldier. The other had made a paper boat, so they stood the soldier in the front and carefully launched it into the gutter.

Swiftly the boat sped along the water until it was swept into a drain beneath the street. The brave tin soldier showed no fear, even when the boat sailed out of the drain and into the river. Then it began to sink!

All too soon the water was up to the soldier's chest. The paper boat became so soggy that it just fell to pieces, and the tin soldier sank beneath the surface.

What a brave tin soldier he was! He showed no fear at all, even when the biggest fish in the river swallowed him up. It was terribly dark and gloomy inside the fish's stomach. The brave tin soldier kept his spirits up by thinking about the lovely ballerina, and how he must see her once more.

One day, the great fish
was caught with a rod and line,
and ended up on a kitchen table.
As the cook cut open the fish with
her sharp knife, the brave tin
soldier fell out onto the table. The
startled cook picked him up and
took him up to the nursery.

Now it was the tin soldier's
turn to be surprised. He found
himself in the very same nursery
with the very same toys: the dolls,
the teddies, all his soldier friends –
and best of all, his lovely
ballerina doll, but neither of them
said one word.

That night, when all was quiet, the brave tin soldier slowly made his way to the cardboard castle. He was going to beg the ballerina to come away with him.

As he reached her side the jack-in-the-box lid flew open, and the goblin pushed the brave tin soldier backwards. How dreadful! The poor tin soldier fell straight into the fire.

Then something very strange happened. The nursery door opened and the sudden draught blew the ballerina doll into the arms of the tin soldier. The fire flared up and they both melted away together in the flames.

Next morning, when the fire had cooled, the
maid came to clear out the ashes. All she found was a
little piece of tin in the shape of a heart.

THUMBELINA

There was once a woman who lived all alone. Her cottage stood by itself in the heart of the countryside, far from neighbours and friends.

She was very lonely and longed for someone to keep her company. "I wish I had a little child of my own," the woman said out loud, as she worked in her garden.

It just so happened that an old witch was passing by and heard her. She fumbled in the folds of her cloak and took out one small seed, "This is a magic seed. Plant it and see what grows." And with that the witch vanished.

As the woman was very fond of flowers, she planted the seed carefully in a pot and placed it on her kitchen window.

In no time at all, a green shoot appeared. By the next day a tall stalk had grown with a flower bud at the top.

When the woman bent down to admire it, the flower bud burst open. Sitting right in the middle of the petals was a tiny girl – no bigger than a thumb.

The woman smiled, "I think I shall call you, Thumbelina."

So tiny was the little girl, that half a walnut shell was just the right size for her bed. Her covers were made of rose petals with a soft rose bud for a pillow. A daisy made a perfect hat, and a violet leaf made a fine umbrella.

The woman took great care to see that her beloved Thumbelina came to no harm.

One warm night as she lay fast asleep in her walnut bed, an ugly toad peered through the window. "She'll make a perfect wife for my son," he croaked. And he grabbed Thumbelina in her walnut shell bed and jumped out of the window.

The ugly toad hopped and hopped far away through the darkness, taking great care not to wake little Thumbelina.

When he reached his home in the mud of the river bank, he showed Thumbelina to his son – who was twice as ugly as his father!

The two toads swam with the walnut shell bed into the middle of the river, and placed it on a lily pad. "Tomorrow you can get married," croaked the old toad to his son.

First thing next morning the toads returned. When Thumbelina peeped out of her bed and saw the ugly pair swimming towards her, she screamed with fright.

All at once, the lily pad began to move, swiftly it floated downstream far away from the angry toads.

Thumbelina had the fish in the river to thank for her lucky escape. They had overheard the toads' dreadful plan, and nibbled away at the lily pad to rescue her.

Thumbelina, still on her lily pad, floated swiftly downstream. At last she came to rest at the water's edge in the long grass.

Just at that moment, a big black beetle flew overhead. He swooped down and carried the tiny girl off into the wood to be his bride.

How the other beetles laughed when they saw Thumbelina. "Where are her wings?" the lady beetles cried. "And why has she only got two legs instead of six?" they scoffed.

All this jeering made the big black beetle feel ashamed of Thumbelina. So he flew away, leaving her alone in the wood.

Happily, the little girl soon found new friends all around her. Squirrels and rabbits came to her with their torn jackets and holey socks to mend. The birds and mice often asked her to baby-sit with their young ones. In return they brought her food. The bees buzzed by with honey and she found juicy berries and nuts everywhere.

All too soon autumn came. The days got shorter and the nights grew dark. Cold winds blew all the leaves from the trees, and Thumbelina shivered with cold in her thin clothes.

Most of her woodland friends had crept into their warm holes for their long winter sleep. Poor Thumbelina was all alone.

A few flakes of snow started to fall, just enough to cover the ground. But to tiny Thumbelina it seemed like deep drifts. Very soon she lost her balance and fell with a bump against a grassy bank.

"Who's that knocking on my door?"
squeaked a friendly fieldmouse, as he held his lantern
high. There in its bright beam he saw Thumbelina,
shivering with cold and very hungry. "Come inside
into my warm parlour and have some food, you poor
creature," the fieldmouse said kindly.

Thumbelina liked the fieldmouse so much, and
found his house so comfortable, that she agreed to
stay all winter.

How quickly the winter months passed by.
Thumbelina cooked and cleaned for the mouse, and in
the long evenings she told him lovely stories.

One afternoon the fieldmouse invited his neighbour, the mole, to tea. The tiny girl baked a chocolate cake, and took great care to serve the visitor properly.

The mole was a handsome fellow, with a black velvet coat and very good manners. To her great surprise, after he had eaten the last piece of cake, the mole asked Thumbelina to marry him.

"I don't want to marry anyone," cried Thumbelina with dismay.

All the same the mole invited Thumbelina to see his house underground. They followed the mole through many dark tunnels and passages. The mole loved to live underground, and never went out in the sunshine. Thumbelina trembled. She would hate to live in the dark and never see the light again.

All of a sudden she stumbled over something soft lying on the floor of the tunnel. "It's only a swallow who has died from the cold," the mole shouted over his shoulder. But Thumbelina was sure she could feel the bird's heart beating.

Later that night, when the fieldmouse was asleep, she fetched a blanket and some warm milk, which soon made the swallow feel better.

She cared for him all winter long. And when spring came, he was ready to fly away.

The swallow pleaded with Thumbelina to fly away with him. "If only I could," she sighed. "But the fieldmouse has begged me to marry the mole tomorrow. He has been so good and kind to me that I must agree." So sadly the two friends parted.

Feeling very unhappy, Thumbelina asked the fieldmouse if she might go out in the sunshine for the last time before she married the mole.

As she stepped outside, the swallow swept down from the sky. This was her last chance of freedom. Thumbelina jumped on the bird's back and the swallow carried her home to her cottage.

At long last everyone was together again and happy once more.